W9-AGP-013

the BAD GUYS

in

MISSION UNPLUCKABLE

IF YOU PURCHASED THIS BOOK WITHOUT A COVER, YOU SHOULD BE AWARE THAT THIS BOOK IS STOLEN PROPERTY. IT WAS REPORTED AS "UNSOLD AND DESTROYED" TO THE PUBLISHER, AND NEITHER THE AUTHOR NOR THE PUBLISHER HAS RECEIVED ANY PAYMENT FOR THIS "STRIPPED BOOK."

TEXT AND ILLUSTRATIONS COPYRIGHT © 2015 BY AARON BLABEY

ALL RIGHTS RESERVED. PUBLISHED BY SCHOLASTIC INC., *PUBLISHERS SINCE 1920*, 557 BROADWAY, NEW YORK, NY 10012. SCHOLASTIC AND ASSOCIATED LOGOS ARE TRADEMARKS AND/OR REGISTERED TRADEMARKS OF SCHOLASTIC INC. THIS EDITION PUBLISHED UNDER LICENSE FROM SCHOLASTIC AUSTRALIA PTY LIMITED. FIRST PUBLISHED BY SCHOLASTIC AUSTRALIA PTY LIMITED IN 2015.

THE PUBLISHER DOES NOT HAVE ANY CONTROL OVER AND DOES NOT ASSUME ANY RESPONSIBILITY FOR AUTHOR OR THIRD-PARTY WEBSITES OR THEIR CONTENT.

NO PART OF THIS PUBLICATION MAY BE REPRODUCED, STORED IN A RETRIEVAL SYSTEM, OR TRANSMITTED IN ANY FORM OR BY ANY MEANS, ELECTRONIC, MECHANICAL, PHOTOCOPYING, RECORDING, OR OTHERWISE, WITHOUT WRITTEN PERMISSION OF THE PUBLISHER. FOR INFORMATION REGARDING PERMISSION, WRITE TO SCHOLASTIC AUSTRALIA, AN IMPRINT OF SCHOLASTIC AUSTRALIA PTY LIMITED, 345 PACIFIC HIGHWAY, LINDFIELD NSW 2070 AUSTRALIA.

THIS BOOK IS A WORK OF FICTION. NAMES, CHARACTERS, PLACES, AND INCIDENTS ARE EITHER THE PRODUCT OF THE AUTHOR'S IMAGINATION OR ARE USED FICTITIOUSLY, AND ANY RESEMBLANCE TO ACTUAL PERSONS, LIVING OR DEAD, BUSINESS ESTABLISHMENTS, EVENTS, OR LOCALES IS ENTIRELY COINCIDENTAL.

LIBRARY OF CONGRESS CATALOGING-IN-PUBLICATION DATA

NAMES: BLABEY, AARON, AUTHOR.
TITLE: THE BAD GUYS IN MISSION UNPLUCKABLE / AARON BLABEY.
OTHER TITLES: MISSION UNPLUCKABLE
DESCRIPTION: NEW YORK : SCHOLASTIC INC., 2017. | SERIES: THE BAD GUYS ; 2 |
SUMMARY: STILL YEARNING TO BE SEEN AS HEROES, WOLF, SHARK, SNAKE, AND PIRANHA SET OUT TO RESCUE TEN THOUSAND CHICKENS FROM A HIGH-TECH CAGE FARM—BUT ONE UNEXPECTED PROBLEM IS MR. SNAKE HIMSELF, ALSO KNOWN AS "THE CHICKEN SWALLOWER."
IDENTIFIERS: LCCN 2016013788 | ISBN 9780545912419
SUBJECTS: LCSH: ANIMALS—JUVENILE FICTION. | RESCUES—JUVENILE FICTION. | CHICKENS—JUVENILE FICTION. | HEROES—JUVENILE FICTION. | CYAC: ANIMALS—FICTION. | RESCUES—FICTION. | CHICKENS—FICTION. | HEROES—FICTION. | HUMOROUS STORIES. | GSAFD: HUMOROUS FICTION.
CLASSIFICATION: LCC PZ7.B52864 BE 2016 (PRINT) | DDC [FIC] DC23
LC RECORD AVAILABLE AT HTTPS://LCCN.LOC.GOV/2016013788

ISBN 978-0-545-91241-9

10 9 8 7 6 5 4 17 18 19 20 21

PRINTED IN THE U.S.A. 23
FIRST U.S. PRINTING 2017

AARON BLABEY

the BAD GUYS in MISSION UNPLUCKABLE

SCHOLASTIC INC.

NEWS FLASH!
PANIC AT THE DOG POUND!
We interrupt this program to bring you a breaking news story.
TIFFANY FLUFFIT is our reporter on the scene. Tiffany, what can you tell us?
CHUCK MELON
6 NEWS

Thanks, Chuck!
Well, there have been SHOCKING scenes at the DOG POUND today.
It seems some kind of CRAZED GANG burst in, smashed down a wall, and then drove away in a very loud hot-rod car, causing 200 TERRIFIED PUPPY DOGS to run away in fright.
6
TIFFANY FLUFFIT
6 NEWS

I have with me **MR. GRAHAM PLONKER**,
Chief of Dog Pound Security.

Mr. Plonker, how would you describe these
MONSTERS?

Uh . . . well . . . it all happened
so fast, but . . . I'm pretty sure
there were four of them . . .

I mean, there was definitely a **WOLF**.

6 NEWS

EXCLUSIVE FOOTAGE!

A really *mean*-looking wolf, with pointy teeth.

And there was a **SNAKE**.

6 NEWS

HAVE YOU SEEN THIS SNAKE?

A very *ugly* snake, who also seemed very cranky for some reason . . .

Uh, then there was a **YOUNG LADY** . . .

. . . or possibly a gigantic **SHARK**. It was hard to tell which . . .

Oh yeah, and there was also some kind of nasty little fish.

Maybe a **SARDINE**.

Not sure.

But, Mr. Plonker, would you say that these *villains* seemed . . .

DANGEROUS?

Oh yes, Tiffany. They're dangerous, all right.

In fact, I'd say we are dealing with some *serious* . . .

BAD
GUYS!

· CHAPTER 1 ·

OK, LET'S TRY THAT AGAIN

What's that guy talking about?
We **SAVED** those puppy dogs!
It was a
RESCUE!
We're the **GOOD GUYS** here!

AND FOR THE LAST TIME,
I AM **NOT** A SARDINE!
I'M A PIRANHA!

See, Wolf? No one is EVER going to believe we're good guys. I'm getting out of here before the cops come looking for us.
Oh, NO you don't, Mr. Snake! We're not going to quit now. We're just getting started.

Don't forget **HOW GOOD** it felt to rescue those dogs!

All we need to do now is make sure that everyone can **SEE** that we're **HEROES**.

We just need to do something **SO AWESOME** that the whole world will sit up and take notice!

THIS!
SUNNYSIDE
CHICKEN
FARM

You want us to break into a chicken farm?
Chickens?
Did you say . . . *chickens*?
A chicken farm? But that little chickie looks happy. She doesn't need to be rescued . . .
Oh, really?

Well, take a look INSIDE
Sunnyside Chicken Farm, fellas.

10,000 CHICKENS!

Stuffed into **TINY** cages!

24 hours a day!

With **NO** sunlight!

And **NO** room to run and play!

But that's awful!
That's the worst thing
I've ever heard!
What are we waiting for?!
WE NEED TO SET THOSE
LITTLE CHICKIE-BABIES
FREE!
Let's go! Let's go! Let's go!
Let's go! Let's go! Let's go!
Let's go! Let's go! Let's go
Let's go! Let's go! Let's go
LET'S GO!

What's up with Mr. Snake?
I don't know. I guess he just really loves chickens.
DROOL!
DROOL!

Well, *helloooo* . . .
Are you OK, man?
Huh?
DROOL

Oh yeah . . . sorry.
I was just thinking that chickens are delicious—I mean, *DELIGHTFUL*—and I think we need to save them all **RIGHT NOW**.
Oh, if only it were that simple, my friend. But I'm afraid I have some bad news . . .

Sunnyside Chicken Farm is

IMPOSSIBLE

to break into!

It's a **MAXIMUM SECURITY CHICKEN FARM** with **STEEL WALLS** that are thirty feet high and eight feet thick!

There are **NO WINDOWS** and all the doors are **HEAVILY GUARDED.**

And even if you *did* get inside, you'd be caught instantly because . . .

If you touch the FLOOR, an **ALARM** goes off!
If you touch the WALLS, an **ALARM** goes off!

And if you walk into the LASER BEAMS, an **ALARM** goes off!

Did you say
LASER BEAMS?
Why are you even showing us this, *chico*? We don't have the skills to pull off a job like this!
No, we don't.
But I know a guy who does.
Who?

ME!

• CHAPTER 2 •

the FREAKY GEEK

Hey, dudes! It's totally awesome to meet you!

Aieeeeee!

RUN, *CHICOS*! It's a **TARANTULA!!!**

Can't breathe . . .
freaking out . . .
don't like . . .
spiders . . .
can't breathe . . .
Are you kidding?

I'm sorry about this, Legs.
I don't know what's
wrong with them.

Aw, it's cool.
Happens all the time.

LEGS?!

You *know* this monster?!

What were you thinking,
bringing a tarantula into
our clubhouse?

Can't breathe . . .
spider . . .
Mommy . . .
Mommy . . .
I want my mommy . . .

Mr. Shark! Pull yourself together!
You guys should be ASHAMED of yourselves!
LEGS is just like us.
He's a GOOD GUY with a BAD reputation.

He's **DANGEROUS,** man.

I don't do pants, dude. I like to feel free.
Can't breathe . . .
no pants . . .
freaking . . . out . . .
Okey dokey.
Legs? Why don't you show them what you can do?

HIGHEST SECURITY
OK. Let's start with something simple.
TAP! TAP! TAP!
TAP! TAP! TAP! TAP!
ACCESS: GRANTED
Name: MR. SNAKE
Status: Very Dangerous
Action: Do Not Approach
Hey! That's my police file!
Geez, they don't like you very much, do they?

But NOBODY can access that! There's no way you can hack into their system. That's the toughest security there is!

Yeah, it *is* kind of tricky.
TAP!
TAP!
TAP!
TAP!
TAP!
TAP!
TAP!
TAP!

But it's worth it just to see you smile, Mr. Snake.

ACCESS: GRANTED
Name: MR. SNAKE
Status: Very Lovable
Action: Give Him a Hug
Ta-da!
That's
IMPOSSIBLE!

Not for a **SUPERHACKER** like Legs! He's a computer **GENIUS**. And he has a plan that will get us inside that chicken farm.
Thanks, Wolfie. But first, I'd better put this back the way I found it. We are good guys, after all . . .
. . . and I wouldn't like to get us in trouble. Sorry, Mr. Snake. You're *dangerous* again, I'm afraid.
Hey!

This is **SO** cool, guys! I'm so happy to be part of the team. And I bet by this time tomorrow, we're totally going to be **BESTIES!**

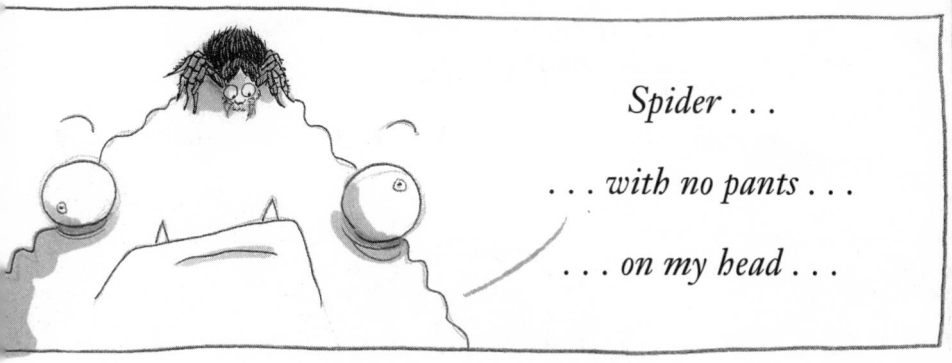
Spider . . .
. . . with no pants . . .
. . . on my head . . .

FAINT!
Hey, *chico*. I got one word for you— *pants.*
SPLAT!

• CHAPTER 3 •

MISSION, LIKE, TOTALLY IMPOSSIBLE

OK, dudes, I took your advice and found myself some clothes. What do you think?

I can still see his
BIG FURRY BUTT.
Cut it out, Piranha. Just listen to him.
OK.
To get you guys inside Sunnyside Chicken Farm, all I need to do is hack into their main computer and switch off all the alarms.
BUT
there's a problem . . .

The security is
SO HIGH
that I can't do it from here.

I need you guys to plug
THIS THING
into their computer,
so I can access it.

Once you do that, I can
SHUT IT ALL DOWN
and get you to those
chickens.

Wait a minute. You're telling
us that you can hack into my
police file, but you **CAN'T**
get into a CHICKEN FARM
without our help?

Yeah. It's WEIRD. This is one SCARY chicken farm, dude.
But if it's so scary, how do we get to the computer? Wolf said there's no way into the building!
Well, there is ONE way.
But it sure isn't easy . . .

There's a **SMALL HATCH** on the roof.

You'll need to go through the hatch and **DROP** 150 feet on a rope to the computer below. Once you get to it, **JUST PLUG ME IN**.

BUT!

If you touch the WALLS or the FLOOR, the **ALARMS** will go off and you'll get caught.

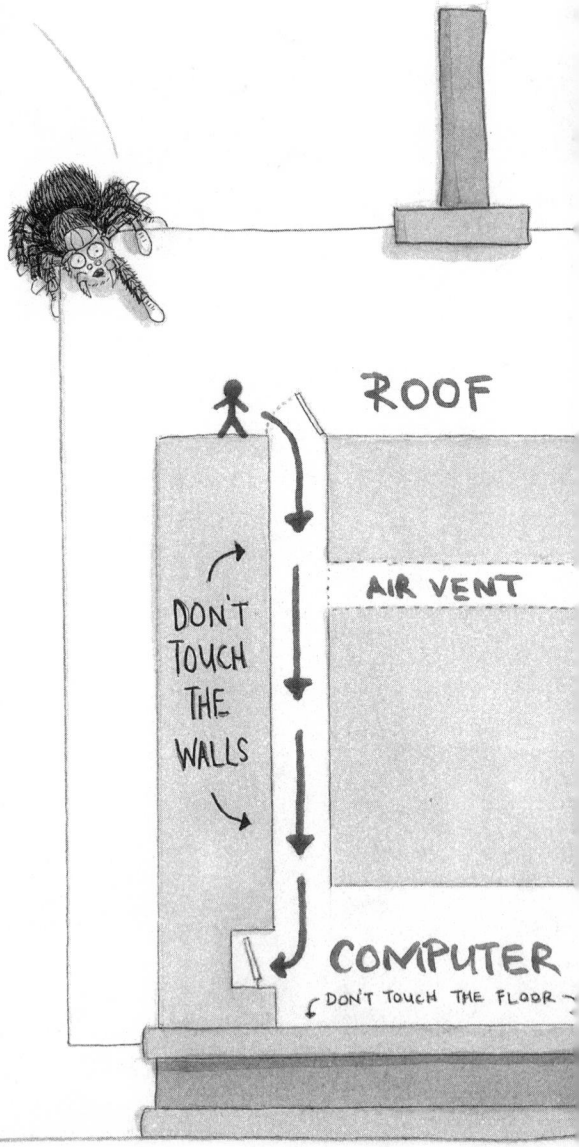

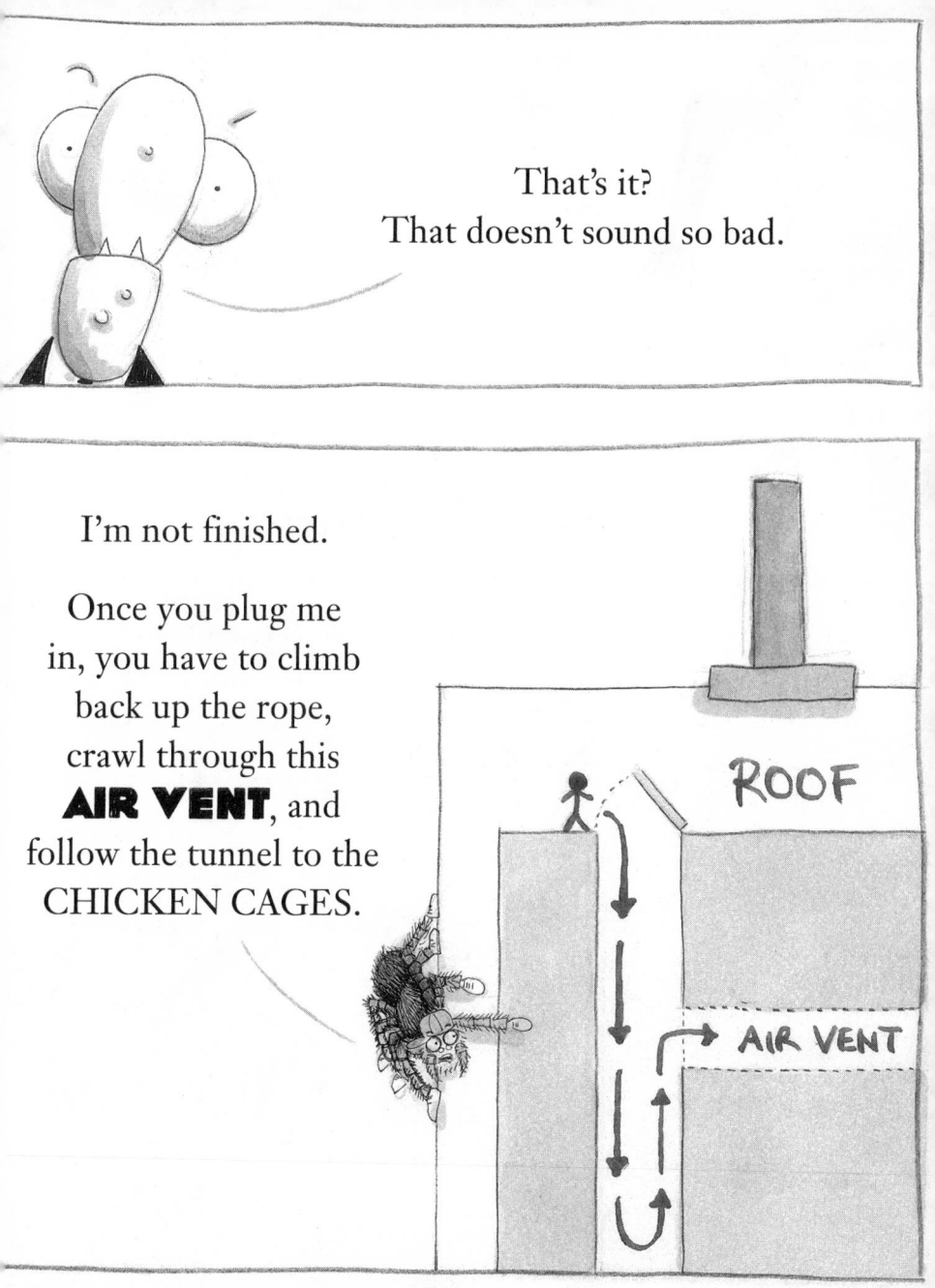
That's it?
That doesn't sound so bad.
I'm not finished.
Once you plug me in, you have to climb back up the rope, crawl through this **AIR VENT**, and follow the tunnel to the CHICKEN CAGES.
ROOF
AIR VENT

Like I said, that doesn't sound so bad.

I'M STILL NOT FINISHED.

You see, before you reach the chicken cages, you'll come to the **LASER BEAMS**. And if you touch one, the alarms will go off.

Oh, and they'll zap you. And they *really* hurt.

But why are the lasers still on? I thought you were going to shut down all the alarms.
I will. The OTHER alarms will be off.
But the LASER ALARMS can only be turned off by hand. You have to flick a switch once you're inside.
So . . . we just switch them off?
Yep.
That *still* doesn't sound so bad.

That's because I'm **STILL NOT FINISHED!**

The switch is on the OTHER SIDE of the laser beams, so you have to GO **THROUGH** THEM to reach it!

You finished yet?
Uhhh . . . yep.
Good! Because that sounds LOCO!
There's NO WAY we can pull this off, man!

Oh yes, we can!

But **ONLY** if we work as a **TEAM!**

So, Snake and Piranha—

you guys are coming with ME!

We are going to **GET INSIDE**,

plug **THIS THING** into the computer, and

GET TO THOSE CHICKENS!

This is going to be

GREAT!

But . . . what about me?
You're going to be working with me, Big Guy.
It's OUR JOB to get these guys in and out of there safely!
Isn't this awesome? You and I are going to SPEND A
LOT OF TIME TOGETHER!
Oh . . . that's . . .
great . . . but . . .
I think . . .
I'm going . . .
to cry . . .

No time for tears, Mr. Shark.

• CHAPTER 4 •
DOWN THE HATCH

Hey, what are you guys doing all the way over there?

LATER THAT NIGHT . . .
SUNNYSIDE
CHICKEN FARM
KEEP OUT!
We look ridiculous.
SUNNYSIDE
INC.

Hey, Tarantula! What's with the stupid suits?

Shhh! Not so loud, Mr. Piranha. These suits are GREAT! They'll keep you cool and make you really hard to spot.
PLUS!
Each suit has a microphone and earpiece, so we can all talk to each other.
GOT IT?

Hey, Wolf, do you really promise there'll be chickens down there?
It's a CHICKEN FARM! Of course there'll be chickens. Why are you so worried about that?
Oh, no reason.
I just really LOVE chickens, man
They're so nice to eat— I mean, they're so nice to *MEET*.
Yeah . . .

You DO understand that we're here to SAVE the chickens, don't you?
Uh-huh.
And you wouldn't try to EAT any chickens, would you?
Uh-uh.
Hey! Can we just DO THIS? My jumpsuit is chafing.

OK. Mr. Shark? You know what to do . . .

Gently lower us on the count of three.
ONE . . .
TWO . . .

EEEE!!!
eeeeeeeeeeee
thr

OK. OK. OK. Well, the walls are a *little* closer than I expected.
Mr. Shark! Whatever you do, make sure you lower us *SLOWLY*.

I hear you.

Do you need a hand, big buddy?
BOING!
EEEEEEEEEEE
FOOF!

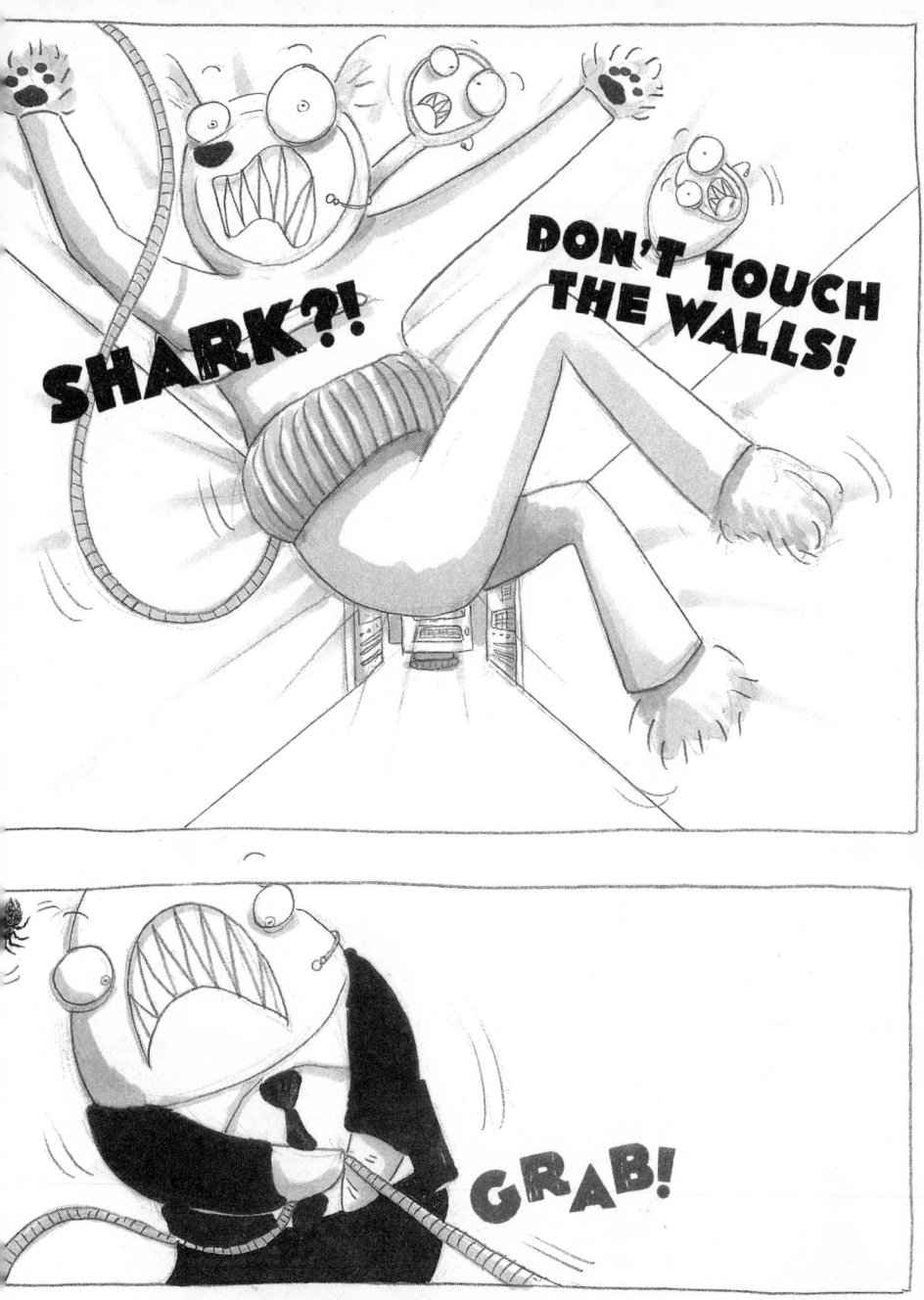
SHARK?!
DON'T TOUCH THE WALLS!
GRAB!

THWACK!
GRAB!
BOING!
DANGLE!
DANGLE!
DANGLE

Whoa. That was close.
¡AY, CARAMBA!
Mr. Wolf?
Has anyone ever told you that your face looks like a BUTT?
What?
Oh. Sorry. My mistake.
Hey, look! The computer! I think I can reach it . . .

This is going to be easier than I thought.
Now, just a little closer and we can plug this thing in . . .

Just a *little* closer.
Uh . . . Wolf?
BUZZZ!

WHISTLE
WHISTLE

He didn't see us.
Why didn't he see us?
Shhh! I don't know.
He must have really bad eyesight.
Um . . . OK . . .
Any suggestions on what we do now?
Are you kidding?
WE GET
OUT OF
HERE!
SHARK?!
ABORT!
ABORT!
PULL US
UP NOW!

Okey dokey . . .
NO! WAIT!
Look what he's eating, *chicos*. That's a sardine sandwich.
I think I have an idea.

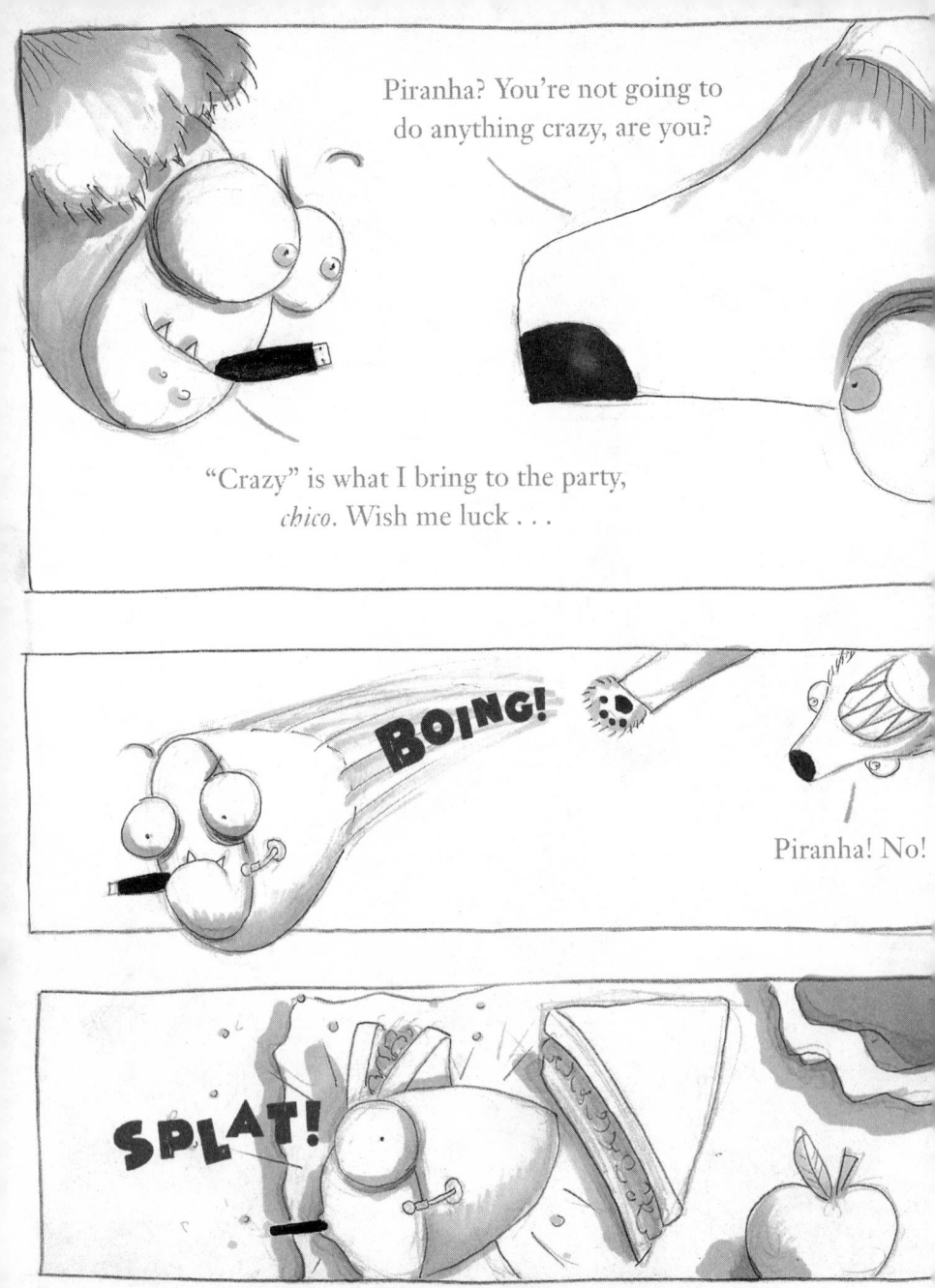
Piranha? You're not going to do anything crazy, are you?
"Crazy" is what I bring to the party, *chico*. Wish me luck . . .
BOING!
Piranha! No!
SPLAT!

WIGGLE!
WIGGLE!
WIGGLE!
CLICK!
I don't believe it! HE DID IT!
He sure did, dudes. I'm in!
And . . .

•ALARMS•
SHUTDOWN
TAP!
TAP!
TAP!
TAP!
TAP!
TAP!
TAP!
The alarms are off! I repeat—the ALARMS ARE OFF! You are safe to enter the AIR VENT.
Piranha! I can't reach you! You'll have to jump . . .
No, Mr. Wolf . . .

This was a one-way ticket, *chico*.
WHAT? We can't just leave you behind!
You have to, *hermanos*. There is no other way.
Go and save those little chickens, man. Save them for **ME!**

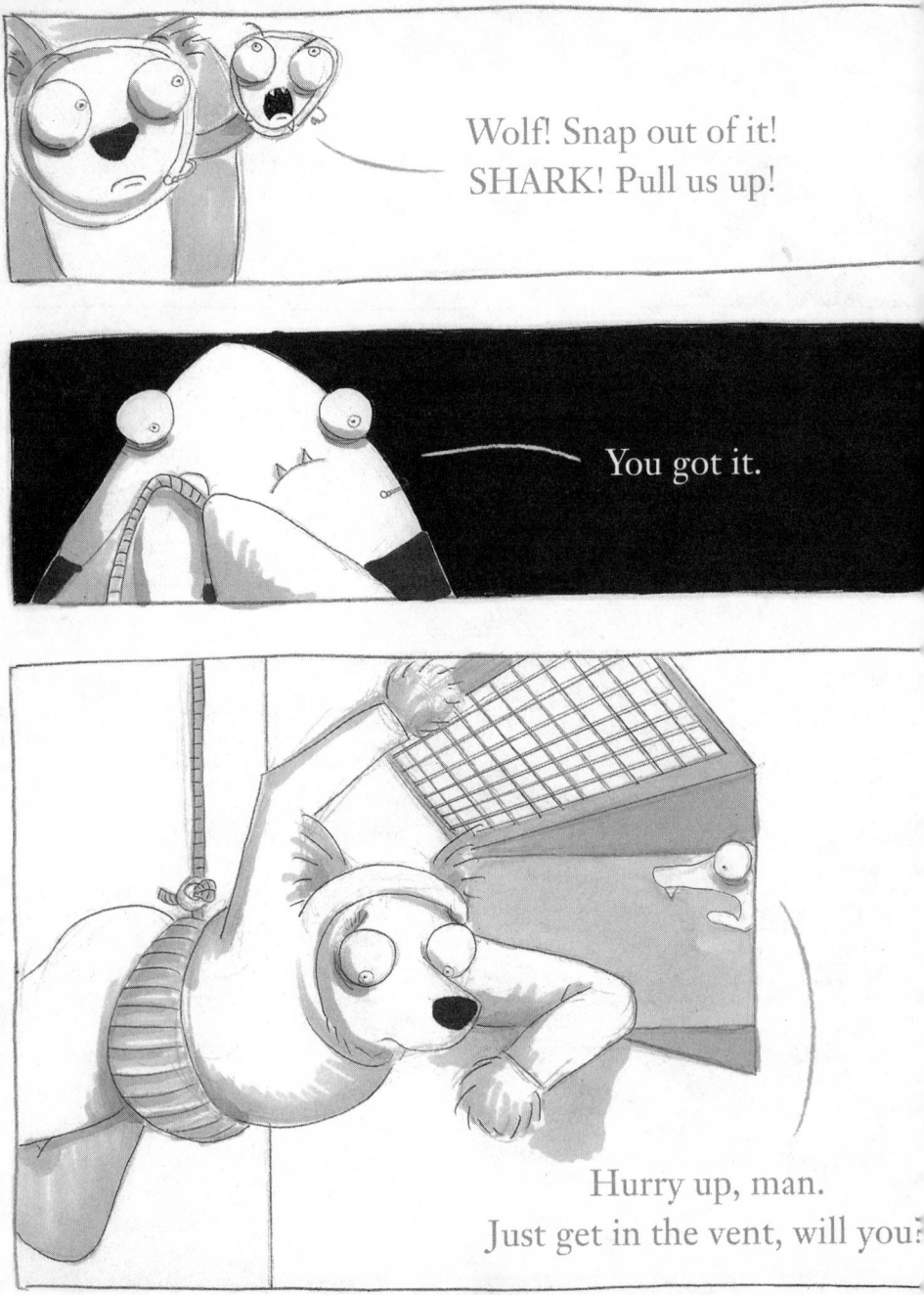
Wolf! Snap out of it!
SHARK! Pull us up!
You got it.
Hurry up, man.
Just get in the vent, will you?

Look at him down there!
What a brave little guy!
He sacrificed himself for us.
Yeah, yeah. Let's do this. I'm starving—I mean, I'm *STARTING* to want to save some chickens. Yep.
You're right. We should go.
Adiós, Mr. Piranha.
Stay safe.
Adiós, chicos.
Easy for you to say, baby.

• CHAPTER 5 •

MIND THE GAP

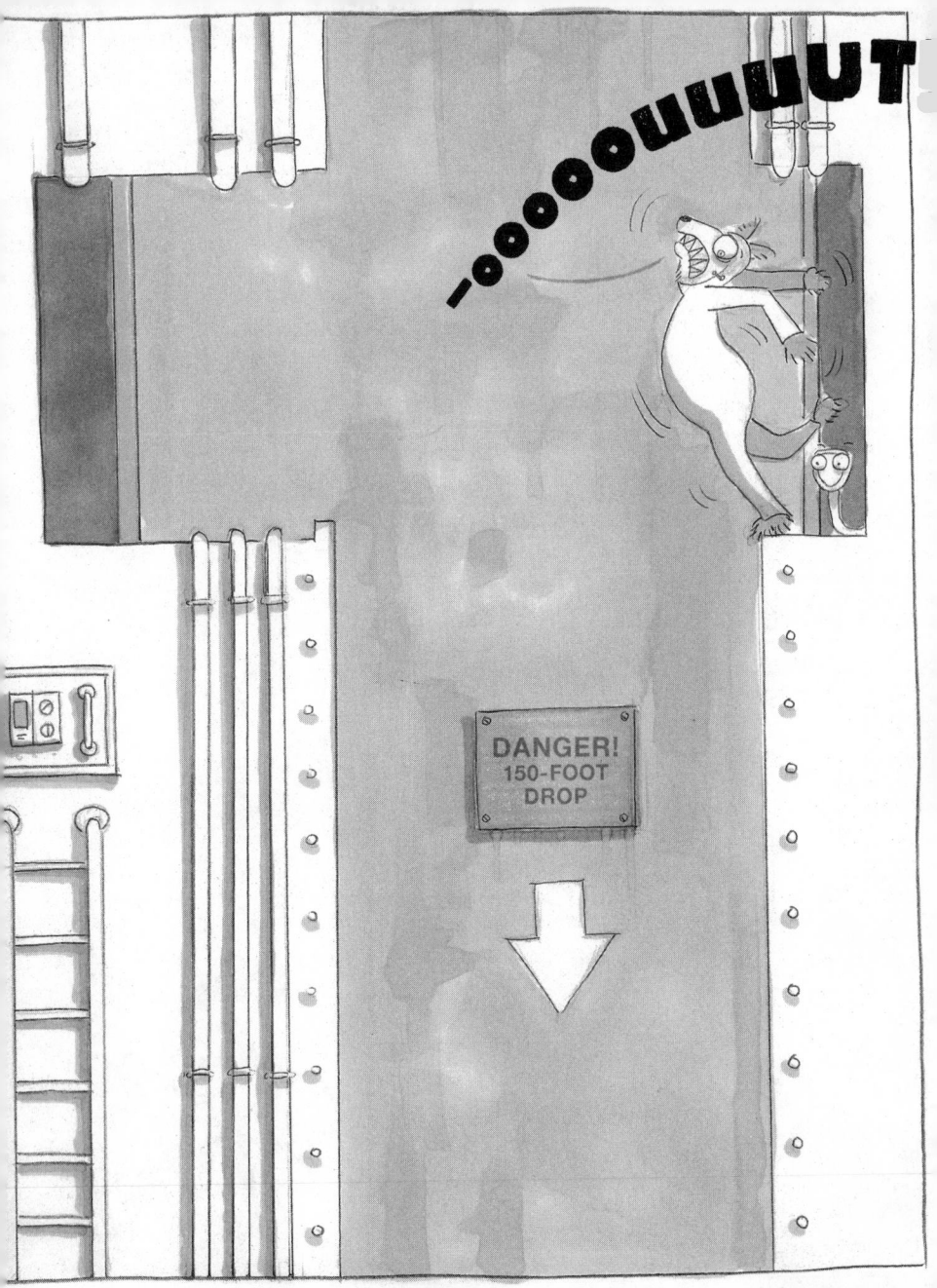
-OOOOOUUUUUT
DANGER!
150-FOOT
DROP

eeEEEEEEEL!
Geez.
If I were you,
I'd try not to
look down.
DANGER!
150-FOOT
DROP
ALL I CAN SEE
IS DOWN!

Hey! I have an idea.
Why don't you stay here?
I'll go and eat—
I mean, *GREET*
those chickens.
Noooo! I'm slipping!
I . . . can't hold on.
You have to . . . help me . . .
Really?
That's a bit annoying.
ANNOYING?!
IF YOU DON'T HELP ME,
I'M GOING TO **DIE!**

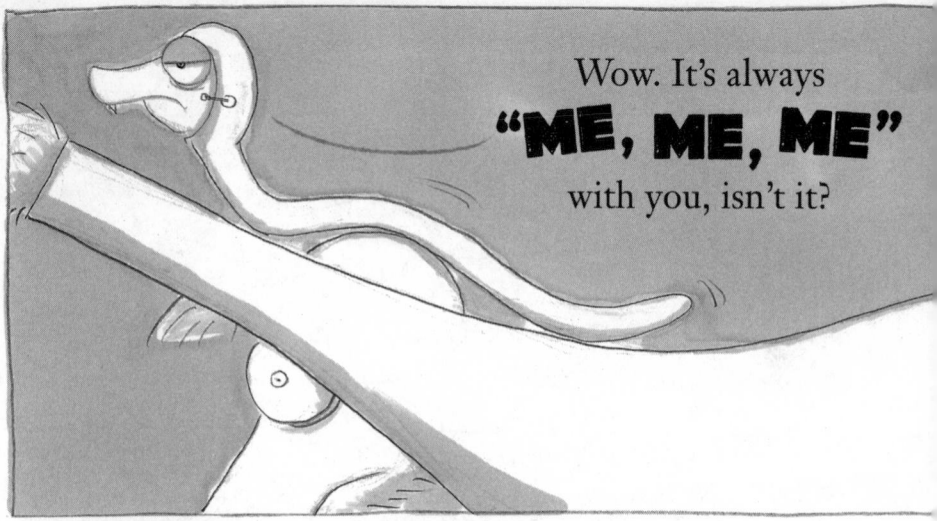
Wow. It's always
"ME, ME, ME"
with you, isn't it?

SLIP!
Oh no!
SLIP!

GRAB!
Hey!
Wait a second.
That's better!

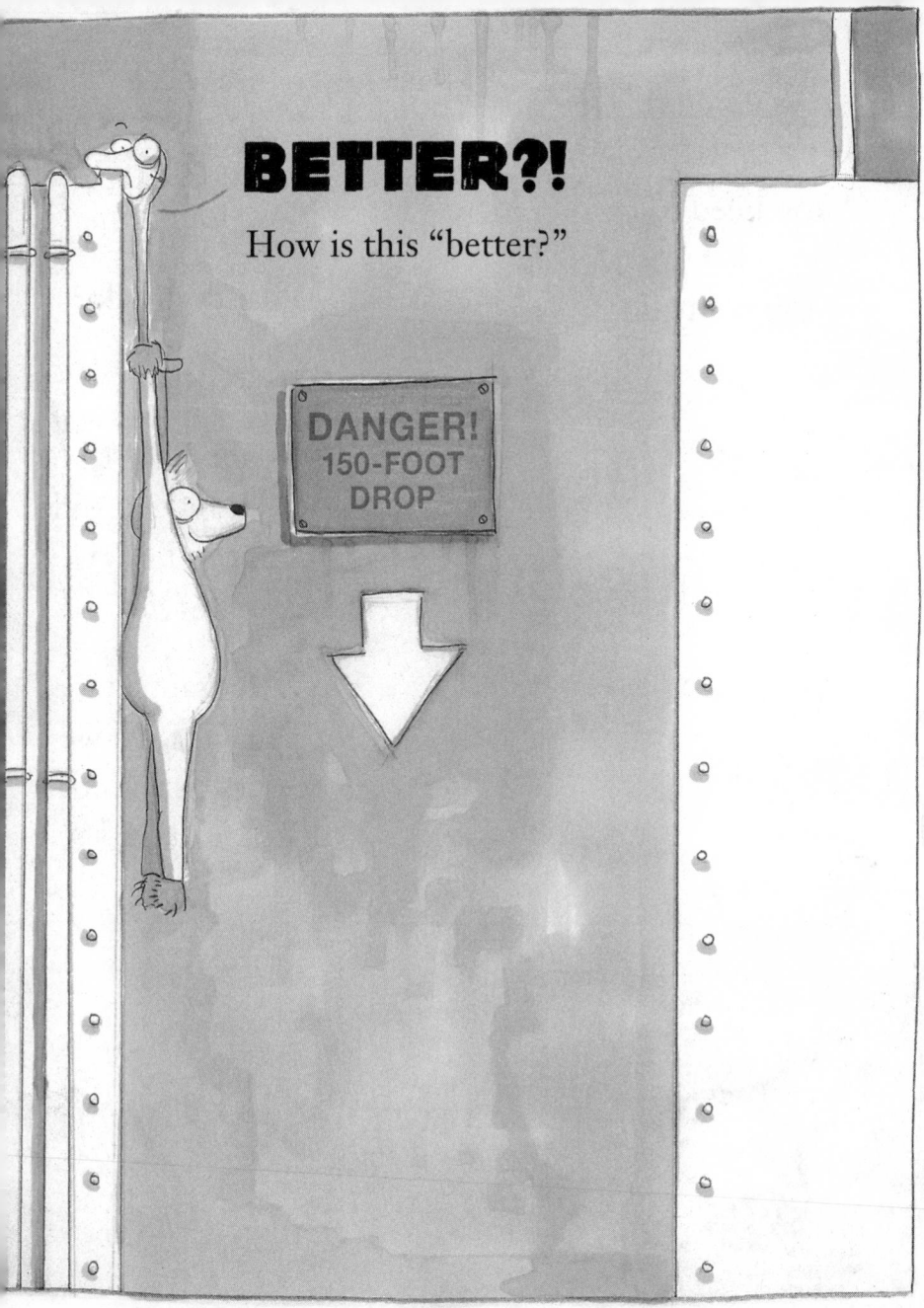
BETTER?!
How is this "better?"
DANGER!
150-FOOT
DROP

You need to go on a diet, man. You really do.

Now, let's think.

What do we do?

We're trapped.

It's not just ME that's trapped. And it's not just YOU. It's **US**.

We're trapped as a **TEAM**. So we need to get out of this as a **TEAM**.

I'VE **GOT** IT!

Now, whatever you do, little buddy . . .
SWING!!
DON'T LET GO!
SWING!!

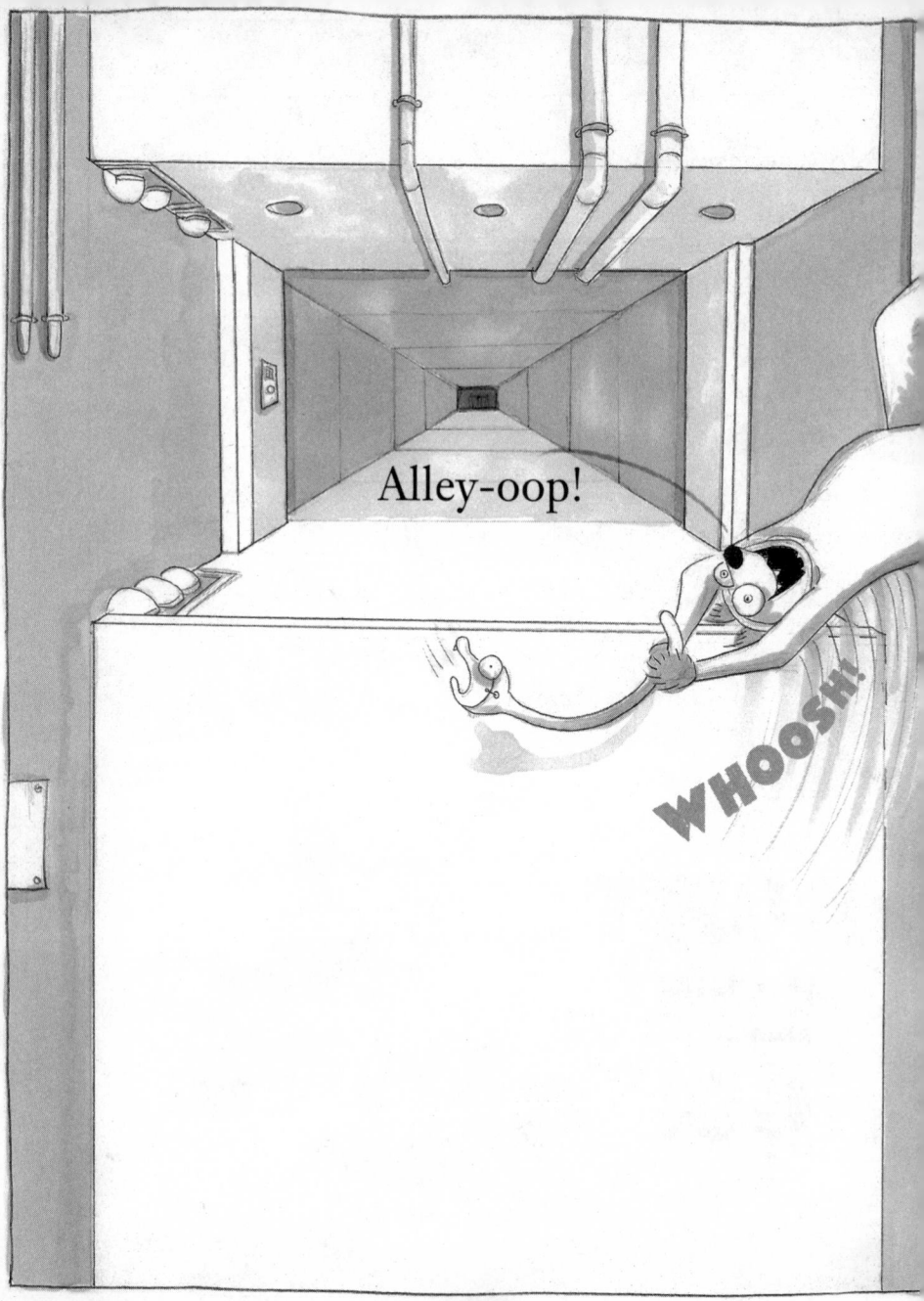
Alley-oop!
WHOOSH!

Ha!
WHOOSH!
THUNK!
BONG!
See? What did I tell you?
Isn't teamwork just GREAT?

• CHAPTER 6 •

LET'S START OVER

Mr. Shark? Is that you?
I'm about to be a monkey's lunch here, man.

You sit tight, Mr. P. I'm coming to get you.

BOING!
Can I help, BIG FELLA?

ARRRRGGGGHHH!
PLEASE don't . . .
can't breathe . . .
please don't . . .
really please don't . . .
can't breathe . . .
Hey, what's your problem, dude?

Really . . . scared . . . of . . . spiders . . .

Uh-huh. And why is that?
It's OK, you can tell me.

OK, well . . .
you're **FREAKY** to look at because
you have **TOO MANY EYES** and
TOO MANY LEGS
and I'm SO creeped
out by you that
I MIGHT
THROW UP!

But . . . I'm sorry if that sounds rude.

It's OK.

No, really. I feel terrible saying that. You must think I'm awful.

No, that's OK.
You seem like a nice guy.
But can I ask you one little thing?

Yes, of course.

Well . . .
since I can't help being a tarantula in the same way
that you CAN'T HELP BEING A
MASSIVE, TERRIFYING SEA MONSTER,
I wonder if you could just
GET OVER IT
and then
MAYBE
I could help you rescue your friend!
Um . . . OK.

I'm so sorry. That was really uncool.

It's OK. That's goo advice.

Well . . . um . . . how are we going to rescue that piranha?
I've heard you're pretty good at disguises. Is that right?

I have my moments.

OK, well, I'm REALLY good at making stuff. So why don't we work together?

OK.

But what kind of disguise is going to get me inside a chicken farm?

Why don't you pull the feathers out of those pillows there, Mr. Shark, and I'll tell you my idea.

• CHAPTER 7 •
TRUST ME, I'M A SNAKE
Oh no! Look at those laser beams! I'll NEVER get through!
I think we have a problem.

CAGE

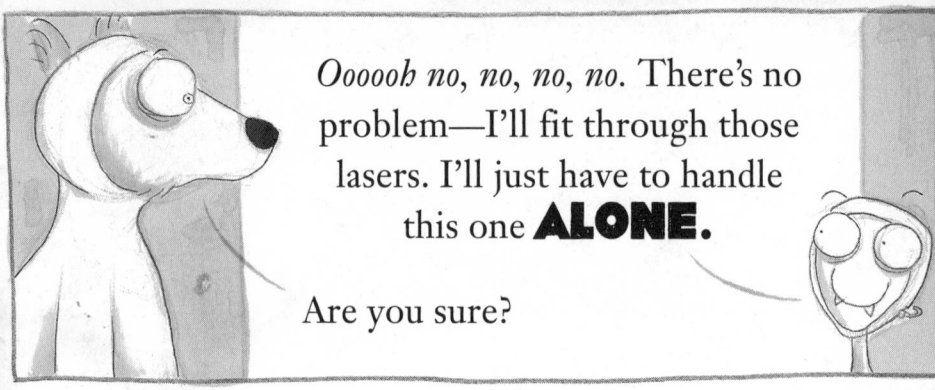
Oooooh no, no, no, no. There's no problem—I'll fit through those lasers. I'll just have to handle this one **ALONE.**
Are you sure?

Oh, ABSOLUTELY. I'll just wriggle my way across and have a chicken feast—I mean . . . I'll get those chickens **RELEASED.**
Yeah. *Released.* Heh heh.

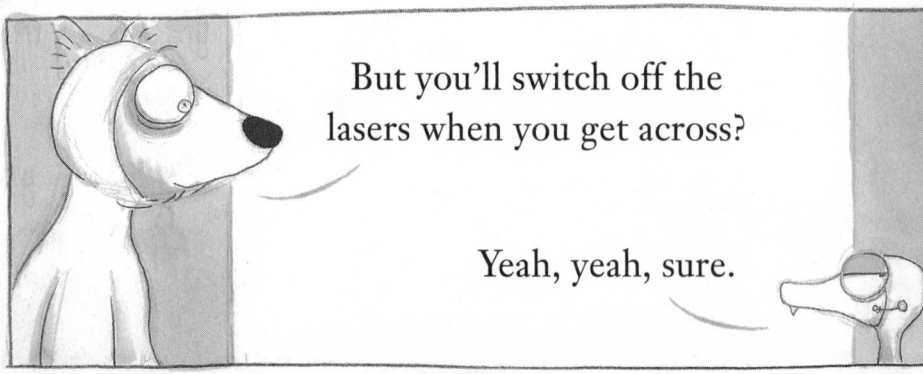
But you'll switch off the lasers when you get across?
Yeah, yeah, sure.

Mr. Snake?
Uh-huh?
This is your moment to do some good.
Yup.
I'm counting on you, buddy.
Okey dokey.

GO BE A HERO, MR. SNAKE!

Just a little farther . . .
Ha!

YOU **MADE** IT!

You're amazing!

Now, just switch off the lasers so I can get across . . .

Hmmm, sure.

Just give me a few minutes to find the switch . . .

You take your time, little buddy!
YOU ROCK!
I'm just SO proud of these guys.
WHISTLE
WHISTLE
Geez, it's been fifteen minutes.
Are you OK over there, Mr. Snake?

CAGES
CLICK!
Aha! He's done it.

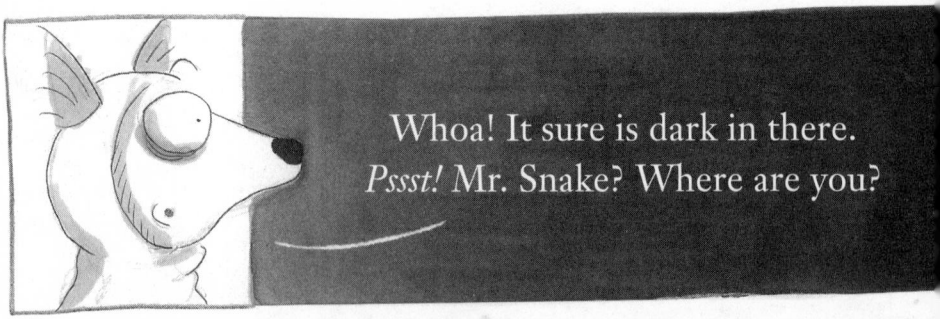
Whoa! It sure is dark in there.
Pssst! Mr. Snake? Where are you?

Oh, there you are!
Is everything OK?
Urghugh.

Mr. Snake?

What are you doing
over there?

In the dark?

Behind all those . . .
EMPTY cages?

You sound funny, man.
Are you OK?

Oh no.

Wait a minute—
You didn't—

SNAKE?!

WHAT DID
YOU DO?!!

Wha—?
OH MY STARS!
ARE YOU FULL OF CHICKENS?!

HEY! YOU TWO!
FREEZE!
!
!
SECURITY
SECURITY

Oh, I don't think so.
Snake, you are *not* going to ruin this plan. No, you are not.
Huh?
GRAB!
NO. YOU. ARE. NOT.

BLUUURRRGGHH!
COUGH THEM UP!

AIIEEEEE!!
KONK!
BONK!

I TRUSTED YOU!
How could you do something so awful?
I'm a SNAKE, man. What did you expect?

NO, Mr. Snake.
YOU ARE A GOOD GUY.
And you're not leaving this building without 10,000 healthy and happy chickens—EVERY SINGLE FLUFFY ONE OF THEM.
ARE YOU FEELING ME?

• CHAPTER 8 •
WHOLE LOTTA CHICKEN

Wow.
That's a big one.
Yeah. I wonder how it got out.

Who knows? But let's get
t back down to the cages.
Oh, sorry!
I interrupted
your lunch . . .
Aw, that's OK.
I can eat on the run.

Hey, *chico*. What's up?
MUNCH!
Clive! Your sardine is alive!
SARDINE?!
That's it, man! Now this little sandwich is going to
EAT YOU!

ARRGGHHH!!!
Yeah, I'm your WORST nightmare, *hombre*! I'm a piranha burger with EXTRA SPICE!
Mr. Shark? Is that you?
Yep.

Wow! I barely recognized you.
Yeah, I know.
I'm good at disguises.
WHOOP! WHOOP! WHOOP!
OH NO! They've set off the alarm!

OP! WHOOP! WHOOP!
But Wolf and Snake will be trapped!

Guys! It's Legs! Get out of there! They're coming for you!

WHOOP! WHOOP! WHOOP!
We're not leaving without our *chicos*.
Or our chickens.

WHOOP! WHOO
The alarm!
We have to hurry!

WHOOP!

We've opened the cages, but they won't run. What's wrong with these stupid chickens?
They're scared.
Of what?
OF THE CREEP WHO TRIED TO EAT THEM!

I couldn't help it.
I'm sorry.
Yeah, well, "sorry" won't help us now, Mr. Snake.
What are we going to do? The chickens are terrified.
They need someone to **FOLLOW**.
They need someone to **TRUST**.
They need . . .

. . . A MOTHER HEN.

Wow. That's one big chicken.

All right, girls. I know you're scared, but this is your ONE CHANCE to get out of this horrible place.
Do you understand?

GOOD
Run, little
chickies! Run!

THEN LET'S GET OUT OF HERE!

Mr. Piranha! You're here!
Are you OK?
I'm completely coated in mayonnaise.
Oh. I see.
It's not too bad, actually.
I kind of like it.

DANGER! DOOR CLOSING!
DOOR CLOSING
OH NO!
They're locking us in!

RUN!

UP
DOWN
Wait! Look! It's that guy up there.
We'll NEVER stop him in time!
DOOR
CLOSING

We're TRAPPED!

This is the END!

My chickens will NEVER be free!

NOT IF I CAN HELP IT!

DOOR CLOSING
Throw me at him! It's your only chance!

That's the craziest thing I've ever heard!

This is my chance to do some good, Mr. Wolf.

But—
THROW ME NOW OR THESE CHICKENS WILL NEVER BE FREE!
DO IT!
And don't miss.
GOT IT?
Got it.

FLING!

ZOOM!
DOWN

Hi. Let's play a game. The first person to open the door doesn't get bitten by a snake.

You win.
UP
THUNK!

Follow me, ladies!
DOOR OPENING
DOOR OPENING
IT WORKED!

Now, can I ask you to please lock all the guards in behind us after we leave?

Yes, we do.

Oh, and if you don't, I **WILL** find out where you live and you **WILL** find me in your bed in the middle of the night.

Do we have a deal?

• CHAPTER 9 •

WHAT A TEAM

I am so proud of you guys!

10,000 chickens are free

because of **YOU!**

I think we're starting to get the hang of this hero thing, fellas.

And that means you, too, Mr. Snake.
OK, Huggy Bear. Let's not make a great big hairy deal out of it.

Aw, sure thing, you old grouch! Let's get out of here . . .

But . . .

What happened to the CAR?!

Oh yeah. While I was waiting for you guys to get back, I fitted it with **MONSTER TRUCK** tires and a **JET ENGINE**. I hope you don't mind?

We don't mind!

And I noticed that you seemed a little cramped in there, Mr. Shark, so I've modified your seat. If you don't like it, I can always put it back the way it was.

I . . . I *love* it, Legs.
You're very thoughtful.
Thank you.
Anytime, Mr. Shark.
Anytime at all.
I'm breathing.
It's all good.
I'm breathing.
It's all good.
I'm breathing.
It's all good.
SQUEAK!
Hey! Did anybody else hear that?

CRACK!
SQUEAK!
SUNNYSIDE INC.
Hmmm.
It seems to be coming from that
CREEPY OLD HOUSE
next to the chicken farm that we . . .
somehow didn't notice. Perhaps it's
a chicken that's lost its way?
I didn't know chickens
could squeak . . .

Nope. My mistake.
There's nothing here. It's empty.
Well, no. It's not
completely empty . . .
MARMALAD
Look!

SQUEAK!

Awww! Look at the widdle guinea pig! What are you doing here all alone?
I think he's named Marmalade. Cute, isn't he?
MARMALADE

Well, Marmalade—we are the GOOD GUYS CLUB. And we have come to set you free!

You take care, little Marmalade. ENJOY YOUR FREEDOM!
See you, little guy.

Good . . . guys?

GOOD GUYS?

And just because they call themselves GOOD GUYS, they think they can

BREAK INTO MY CHICKEN FARM AND SET MY CHICKENS FREE?!

AND THEY THINK THEY CAN GET AWAY WITH IT?

Well, we'll see about that. I shall make them pay.

Oh yes . . .

I SHALL MAKE THEM PAY! HEHEHEHEHE! HEHEHEHE!

Boy, did these guys mess with the
WRONG
guinea pig!
See what happens when the Bad Guys get captured by a REALLY bad guy.
How will they escape from his evil lair?
Who is that mysterious NINJA that seems to be following them? And when will they all stop trying to EAT each other?!
Don't miss their next so-funny-you'll-wet-your-pants adventure-
the BAD GUYS in
The Furball Strikes Bac
The Bad Guys are about to have a *really* BAD day . . .